GREATEST Magical STORIES

Chosen By
MICHAEL MORPURGO

This book belongs to:

_____

OXFORD
UNIVERSITY PRESS

Great Clarendon Street, Oxford OX2 6DP

Oxford University Press is a department of the University of Oxford.
It furthers the University's objective of excellence in research, scholarship,
and education by publishing worldwide. Oxford is a registered trade mark
of Oxford University Press in the UK and in certain other countries

British Library Cataloguing in Publication Data

Data available

ISBN: 978-01-9-276403-4

1 3 5 7 9 10 8 6 4 2

Paper used in the production of this book is a natural,
recyclable product made from wood grown in sustainable forests.
The manufacturing process conforms to the environmental
regulations of the country of origin.

GREATEST
Magical
STORIES

Chosen By
MICHAEL
MORPURGO

OXFORD
UNIVERSITY PRESS

Introduction

Amongst the first stories most of us ever hear are *Cinderella* or *Sleeping Beauty* or *Jack and the Beanstalk*. These and other magical stories stay with us all our lives. We hear them, read them, see them in one theatrical form or another, again and again. And they have stood the test of time, that's for sure. For centuries children have grown up loving these stories. They are almost part of our DNA. They are universal, loved in countries all over the globe, retold, adapted, for each new age. Grown-up children, parents, grandparents, teachers, have such wonderful memories of living these stories in their minds' eye when they were young, of hearing them from their parents or grandparents or teachers, that they want their own children to grow up with them and love them just as much.

So what is the magic of these stories? How does the spell manage to work for generation after generation, and go on working across the centuries? And why do children love them so much? Well, children are brilliant at suspending disbelief. And that is because they *want* to believe. Actually we all do! They, we, want to believe that good will triumph over evil, right over wrong, that good deeds will be rewarded. We long for our hopes to be fulfilled—for the little girl so cruelly bullied by her sisters and stepmother in Cinderella to find her prince, to find love and happiness; for her whole horrible family to get their just deserts. They, we, want to believe the impossible—that a magic bean can grow into the tallest beanstalk there ever was, right up into the clouds; that Jack is not frightened to climb it, not frightened by the nasty wicked giant. Jack will sort him out, put an end to him somehow, and one way or another he will manage to escape, and all will end happily ever after.

Every one of these stories is like that magic bean. Each of them grows in our mind as we read, and we wonder where it will take us if we climb it. And climb it we must, if we want to find out what is at the top and what will happen when we get there. So climb into these stories, but look out for wicked giants and nasty wolves that dress up as grandmothers.

Michael Morpurgo

Contents

Have you ever looked out to the sea and wondered what mysterious creatures live beneath the waves? For hundreds of years people in Scotland have been telling stories and singing songs about magical sea-creatures like kelpies, selkies, mermaids, and mermen. This story is about two children who find themselves trapped in the palace of the wicked and greedy Merman Rosmer, who claims that 'once the salt gets into your blood, you can never go back to land'.

The Merman

Retold by Malachy Doyle

Illustrated by Victoria Assanelli

One winter morning little Sylvie was down by the water, singing to the seals. From under the sea, a merman spotted her.

'What a bonny lassie,' he said. 'I will take her to my home beneath the waves, and keep her there. For once the salt gets into her blood, she can never go back to land.'

The merman reached out a long, long arm. He picked
Sylvie up and carried her over the sea to his island.

Sylvie's mother wept for her lost
daughter.
'Don't cry, Mother,' said Sylvie's
brother Peter. 'I will fetch her home.'

Peter sat in his little rowing boat, ready
to sail the salty sea.

'Take care, my love,' said his mother.
'I've lost poor Sylvie. I don't want
to lose you as well.'

Young Peter rowed, all day and all
night, till he came to the merman's island.
He went into a cave, then down, down,
down till he came to a great palace.

Peter found Sylvie in the kitchen of the palace,
making porridge for the merman's breakfast.

'Oh Peter!' she cried. 'I'm so happy to see you! But
you must hide before he finds you.'

When the merman came in, Sylvie said, 'A little
fisher boy has come over the salty sea to visit me.
You won't harm him, will you?'

'Not if you don't want me to,' said Merman Rosmer, for that was his name.

But he wouldn't let Peter go home. 'You must stay here, laddie, and be my servant,' said the merman. 'For once the salt gets into your blood, you can never go back to land.' But the children wanted to go home!

One morning, Sylvie said to the merman, 'I had the saddest dream last night. The little fisher boy's mother was crying and crying. Please take him back to her—it is the only thing that will make me happy.'

'Very well, for I do so want you to be happy,' said the merman. He had grown to love Sylvie, in his salt-bitter way.

'As well as taking him back, you should bring his mother a present,' the girl told him. 'But only a small one,' she added, 'for I know you're not rich.'

'I am richer than any human!' cried the merman.

He took Sylvie to his treasure room and filled an enormous chest with gold for the fisher boy's mother.

In the night, while the palace shook with the merman's snores, Sylvie crept back to the treasure room. She took all of the gold out of the chest and climbed inside it.

Then she closed the lid and waited . . .

In the morning, Merman Rosmer grabbed young Peter and the chest, and swam over the salty sea to the boy's home.

'Away and find your mother, fisher laddie,' he said, leaving them on the rocks. 'I'm off back to my beloved Sylvie.'

'Mother! Mother!' cried Peter. 'I'm home!'

The children's mother wept for joy at the sight of him.

'But what about my darling Sylvie?' she gasped. 'Did you find her?'

'I found a treasure chest . . . ' said the boy. And he led her down to the rocks.

The children's mother opened the
box . . . and out jumped Sylvie!

As all three hugged, they heard an angry roar
from the ocean. The children and their mother
raced away from the waves which rushed towards
them. They ran and ran, and kept on running.

19

And it was as well they did. Merman Rosmer was very angry that his beloved Sylvie had escaped! He sent giant waves to smash her house, till each and every wall tumbled to the ground.

The children's mother built another home, far inland. And from that day on, she, Sylvie, and Peter stayed clear of the salty sea. They'd escaped before, but they might not again. For you know what they say—once the salt gets into your blood, you can never go back to land.

It's never nice to be left out of the fun, but I think it's fair to say that the fairy in this story overreacts a little when she doesn't get her invite to the royal party. In an act of revenge she curses Princess Aurora to 100 years of sleep! No matter how hard Aurora's parents try they can't escape the fairy's magic, but there is one way to break the curse . . .

Sleeping Beauty

Retold by Pippa Goodhart

Illustrated by Bee Willey

Once upon a time, a king and queen wanted a child. When the Queen gave birth to a baby girl, they were proud and happy.

'We must give her a truly lovely name,' said the Queen.

'And we must have a grand party,' said the King. 'Everyone will want to come and see her.'

They thought of lots of names for their baby. At last they found just the right one.

'She was born at dawn,' said the Queen. 'So we should call her Aurora. Aurora means "the dawn".'

'Perfect!' said the King. 'And her party shall be perfect too.'

The King wrote invitations to lots of people.

'I will invite the fairies, because fairies can give our daughter the best gifts of all,' he said. The King found the names of seven fairies. 'Seven is a lucky number, so that's good,' said the King.

The party was lit with lanterns, and there was music from trumpets and drums. Everyone was dressed in wonderful clothes. There was a feast of food served on gold plates, and the seven fairies ate using diamond-studded knives and forks.

Princess Aurora lay in her cradle. All the guests were happy and laughing and eating.

'Oh, this is perfect!' said the King.

'Just perfect,' said the Queen.

But just then . . . **CRASH!**

The door opened. Wind swirled into the room. There, on the doorstep, stood a nasty-looking fairy.

The music and laughter stopped.

'Why was I not invited to this party?' said the nasty fairy.

'Oh dear. You should have been!' said the King, hurrying to bring the fairy into the party. 'I am so sorry, Madam Fairy. I didn't know about you, so I couldn't invite you. But I invite you now. Do sit down.'

The King himself laid a new place at the table for the nasty fairy. But he didn't have more knives and forks with diamonds in. She was given plain gold ones.

'So I am not as welcome as those other fairies?' said the nasty fairy.

'Oh dear, oh dear,' said the Queen.

The fairies began to give their gifts. One by one they came forward.

'My gift will give you beauty,' said the first fairy, waving her wand over baby Aurora.

'My gift will make you clever,' said the second fairy.

The next four fairies gave Aurora gifts to make her kind and caring, and to make her good at dancing and singing.

But then . . . **BANG!**

That nasty fairy hit the floor with her stick.

'You've forgotten me again!' she said. She pointed at baby Aurora. 'My gift to you is that one day you will prick your finger on a spindle, and you will die!'

'No!' said the Queen.

'Now you see why you should have invited me!' said the nasty fairy.

But there was still the youngest fairy who hadn't yet given her gift.

'I don't have the power to undo that bad spell,' she said. 'But my gift is to make Aurora sleep for a hundred years rather than die.'

Well, that was
the end of the party.

The King ordered every spindle in
the kingdom to be burned. He got
a nanny to keep a close watch on
Princess Aurora. He made very sure
that she was safe as she grew up. For
sixteen years all went well.

But when Aurora was no longer a child, her nanny left. There came a day when the King and Queen were out for a visit, and Princess Aurora thought, *Now I'm going to explore the whole palace!*

Aurora climbed up a turret where she had never been before. At the top she found a room with an old lady in it. This old lady had never heard of the King's rule about spindles.

'What are you doing?'
asked Aurora.

'I am spinning thread,'
said the old lady, giving her
spindle a twist.

'Please may I have
a go?' asked Aurora.
Of course Aurora had
never seen anybody
spinning before. She
reached out a finger
. . . and pricked it on
the spindle spike.

Straight away, Aurora fell fast asleep onto the floor. The old
lady couldn't wake Aurora, so she called for help.

When the King and Queen came home, they were
very upset.

'We shouldn't have left her alone,' they said. They got
a doctor to try and wake Aurora. They tried slapping her
hands. They put cold water on her face.

Nothing woke her. 'I think we must send for that kind
young fairy again,' said the Queen. 'She will help us.'

The kind fairy came, and she told them, 'Aurora will sleep

for a hundred years. But it will be so sad for her to wake up after all that time, and find that you have died. So shall I make you all sleep too?'

'Oh, yes,' said the King and Queen. 'We want to be here when she wakes.'

The kind fairy touched the King and the Queen with her wand. 'Sleep now for as long as Aurora sleeps,' she said.

She touched her wand to all the servants
and animals too. Everything living
in the palace slept, even the fires and
fountains.

The kind fairy promised Aurora,
'A prince will wake you from your sleep
when the time is right.'

As the kind fairy left the palace, she
touched her wand to a tree outside. A
great thick forest of trees and thorns
grew around the palace to keep Princess
Aurora safe.

For a hundred years everything in that palace slept. Outside, the world went on as usual. From time to time somebody would ask, 'What is behind that big hedge of thorns?'

At first people knew the answer.

'A princess sleeps there, along with the King and Queen and everyone else. After a hundred years they will all wake up.'

Some people thought, I will go and rescue them! But everyone who tried to hack through the hedge found that they could not. Those magic thorns were strong.

As time passed, the stories changed.

'There's something behind the hedge. See those turrets? It must be a castle. I think an ogre lives there. Or ghosts.'

But one day a young prince called Florimond came riding into the forest. He didn't believe the stories about an ogre or ghosts.

At last he found an old woodcutter who told him, 'Well there is another story. My grandfather told it to me. He said that there is a beautiful princess asleep, and only a kiss from a prince can wake her.'

'Well I am a prince!' said Prince Florimond.

So Prince Florimond pulled out his sword and he hacked at the trees. This time the trees magically opened up a path in front of him. Florimond walked into the palace full of sleepers.

He looked all around, and at last he found sleeping Princess Aurora.

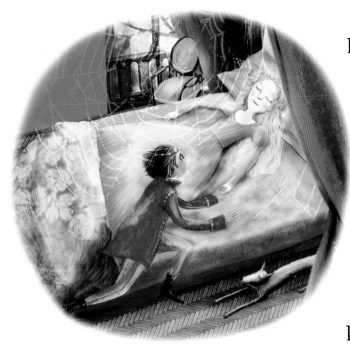

'You truly are beautiful,' he told her. 'Would you mind if I kissed you?'

Of course, Princess Aurora couldn't answer.

'I will only kiss your hand,' said Prince Florimond. He gently lifted her hand, and he kissed it.

And Princess Aurora woke.

'Hello!' said Aurora, rubbing her eyes. 'Who are you?'

As Aurora and Florimond talked, everyone in the palace awoke. The fires came to life. Water in the fountain flowed. The cooks got cooking. Gardeners picked flowers. Dogs barked. The King and Queen hurried to find their daughter.

'This is Prince Florimond,' Princess Aurora told them. 'He woke us all up.'

'In that case he must stay for dinner!' said the King.

Prince Florimond didn't just stay for dinner. He stayed for days and weeks. They all liked him very much. Princess Aurora liked him the best of all. It wasn't long before she decided to marry him.

They had the grandest of weddings. The King wrote the invitations. How many fairies do you think he invited to the wedding party?

Eight! The nasty fairy was given the best of everything at the party. That made her happy, and almost nice. So she gave Aurora and Florimond a wonderful wedding present . . . if you like that sort of thing!

The Frog Prince is a very old tale, first written down by the Brothers Grimm. It tells the story of a princess who promises to be friends with a talking frog after he rescues her ball from a pond. Luckily, unlike other famous versions of the tale, the princess doesn't have to kiss the frog; but she does have to learn the importance of keeping a promise.

The Frog Prince

Retold by Pippa Goodhart

Illustrated by Yannick Robert

Long ago and far away, there lived a princess.
On her birthday the Queen said, 'I promise to give you any toy you want.'

'I want a ball made of gold,' said the Princess.

'There are no balls made of gold,' said the Queen.

'But a promise is a promise,' said the Princess.

So the Queen had a ball of gold made for the Princess.

One day the Princess was playing with her ball. But the ball fell into the pond.

'I have lost my ball made of gold!' said the Princess. She began to cry.

A small frog hopped over to the Princess.

'I can get your ball back,' the frog said.

'Frogs can't talk!' said the Princess.

'Well I can!' said Frog.

'I will get your ball back,' said Frog.
'But only if you make me a promise.'

'I will promise anything you like,' said the Princess.
'You can even have my crown!'

'A frog has no need for a crown,' said Frog.

'What *do* you want, then?' said the
Princess.

'I want you to promise to be my
friend,' said Frog.

'Easy!' said the Princess. 'I will do that.'

So Frog jumped into the pond. He got
the ball back, just as he had promised.

'Now we will be friends,' he said.

The Princess grabbed the ball. She did not say 'thank you' to Frog.

'Hey!' said Frog. 'What about your promise?'

But the Princess just ran away.

Later, as the Princess ate her supper, she heard a sound.

'What's that?' said the Queen.

'Nothing,' said the Princess.

'Open the door!' said the Queen.

'No, please don't!' said the Princess.

The Queen opened the door.

'Oh no!' said the Princess. Frog came into the room.

'Good evening,' he said.

'What do you want, Frog?' said the Queen.

'I want the Princess to be my friend, just as she promised,' said Frog.

'I can't be friends with a cold, wet frog!' said the Princess.

'A promise is a promise,' said the Queen.

So Frog sat at the table and ate supper from a plate made of gold.

'Now will you go back to the pond?' said the Princess.

'A real friend would let me stay,' said Frog.

'A promise is a promise.'

So the Princess took Frog up to her bedroom.

'You can sleep in this nice box,' said the Princess.

'A real friend would let me sleep on her pillow,' said Frog.

So the Princess put Frog on her pillow. As he sat on the pillow, magic happened.

Frog grew and grew. He changed into . . . a boy!

'Who *are* you?' said the Princess.

'I am a prince,' said the boy. 'A witch turned me into a frog. The only thing that could turn me back into a prince was somebody being a good friend to me.'

'But I was a bad friend,' said the Princess. 'I didn't like you at first.'

'You were a good friend,' said the Prince. 'You gave me food. You even let me sit on your pillow.'

The Princess and the Prince became real friends. They liked to play with the ball made of gold, but they never went near the pond.

When they grew up, the Prince and Princess got married.

They promised to love each other for ever. And they did love each other for ever and ever.

After all, a promise is a promise.

In this snowy Norwegian fairy tale, a brave girl called Astrid must overcome many challenges in order to save her prince. Along the way she encounters extraordinary transformations, powerful spells, and enchanted castles—all ingredients for the perfect magical story.

East of the Sun, West of the Moon

Retold by Chris Powling

Illustrated by Violeta Dabija

Long ago and far away, in a land of trolls and magic, there lived a poor farmer. His house was falling down, his family were in rags, and his money was almost gone. Now winter was coming on . . .

'Listen to the wind and the rain!' the farmer wailed. 'What can I do? Won't somebody please help me?'

TAP! TAP! TAP!

There, at the farmhouse door, stood a big white bear.

'I'm lonely,' the bear said. 'Lend me Astrid, your daughter, and I'll make you and your family rich.'

'Rich?' said the farmer.

'Very rich,' said the bear. 'I'll look after her well, I promise. Tell me on Thursday if you agree.'

Well, the family was so poor they had to agree. On Thursday, Astrid found herself clinging to the bear's stiff white fur as he padded away from the farmhouse.

All day long they travelled.
Then, as night fell, they came to
a steep cliff. Or was it the wall
of a castle? Soon they were in a
splendid hall made of the finest
gold and silver.

'Take this bell, Astrid,' said the
bear. 'If there is anything you
want, just ring it.'
'All I want is a soft bed and
sweet dreams,' Astrid yawned.

58

That night she dreamed of a handsome young prince who sat beside her bed while she slept. The same thing happened the next night, and the night after that.

All day long Astrid rang the bell for anything she wanted. And all night long the Prince sat beside her in her dreams.

On the fourth day, Astrid sent for the bear.

'I'm homesick,' she told him. 'I want to see my family.'

'Will you promise to come back?'
said the bear. 'And will you promise not to share any secrets
with your mother?'

'I promise, Bear.'

So the bear took Astrid home.

Astrid's first promise was easy. Her family was now rich and happy so she knew she must stay with the bear.

Her second promise was harder. In a land of trolls and magic, a girl can't help sharing secrets with her mother.

'I dreamed of a prince every night,' said Astrid. 'Or was he real all along?'

'Ah ...' her mother smiled. 'Next time, light this magic candle. But don't spill any magic wax on him!'

'I won't!' Astrid laughed.

Astrid loved the visit to her family. But now she had a plan, she was keen to get back to the castle.

That night, at the gold and silver castle, Astrid went to bed very early. She kept her eyes shut tight until she heard somebody sit beside her bed. Then she lit the magic candle . . . much too quickly.

The Prince was real all right. As real as the three drops of magic wax Astrid had spilled on his shirt.

'Oh, Astrid,' he groaned. 'What have you done? A troll called Long Nose put a spell on me. By day I'm a white bear and by night a royal prince. Now you've spilled some magic, the spell can't be broken. I'll have to marry Long Nose!'

'How can I save you?' Astrid sobbed.

'You can't,' said the Prince, sadly. 'Long Nose will lock me in her castle until our wedding day. It lies east of the sun and west of the moon, so nobody can find me.'

'I can still try . . .' said Astrid.

Next morning, the Prince and the castle had vanished. So had all of Astrid's fine clothes. Dressed in her old rags, she set off at once.

'East of the sun and west of the moon . . . she said. 'Somebody must know where Long Nose lives.'

She walked and walked and walked.

At last, on top of a
high mountain, she
met an old hag.

'I've never heard of Long Nose,' the old hag said. 'You'd
better ask my big sister who lives on the next mountain.
Here, take this golden apple to bring you good luck.'
'Thank you,' Astrid said.

The old hag's sister was no help at all.

'I've never heard of Long Nose,' she said. 'You'd better ask my other sister who lives on the next mountain. Here, take this golden comb to bring you luck.'

'Thank you,'
Astrid said.

But the third old hag shook her head as well.

'I've never heard of Long Nose,' she said. 'My sisters were silly to send you. Here, take this golden spinning wheel to bring you good luck.'

'Thank you,' Astrid said.

Now she was all alone again, with a golden apple, a golden comb, and a golden spinning wheel to carry.

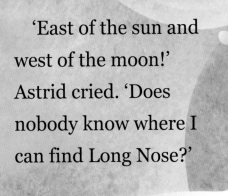

'East of the sun and west of the moon!' Astrid cried. 'Does nobody know where I can find Long Nose?'

'I do,' hissed the East Wind.

'Can you take me there, sir?' Astrid asked eagerly.

'Only if my brothers help me, Astrid: the West Wind,
the South Wind, and the North Wind.'

'Please,' Astrid begged.

So the East Wind swept her into the air. She flew from
wind to wind; East to West to South to North, over hills
and seas and forests.

Then the North Wind set her down.

'Thank you, winds,' said Astrid. 'But where is it you've lifted me?'

'East of the sun and west of the moon,' the North Wind smiled. 'This is where Long Nose lives.'

'Goodbye!' waved Astrid as he gusted off.

Astrid was standing by the
biggest and gloomiest castle
she'd ever seen. Long Nose
was looking down from a high
window.

'Hello, Astrid,' she cackled.
'Are you looking for the Prince?
Give me that golden apple and
I'll let you see him.'

'Take it,' said Astrid,
quickly.

Inside the castle, she found the Prince in a deep, deep
sleep. He was holding an empty silver cup.

'Was that a magic drink?' Astrid wondered. 'If it was,
I'll never wake him.'

The Prince slept all night long.

The next day, Astrid offered Long Nose the golden comb.

'It'll be yours forever,' she said, 'if you'll let me visit the
Prince again.'

'Why not?' sniffed Long Nose. 'I shall keep him fast asleep until our wedding day!'

So it was a magic drink in the silver cup . . .

That night, while the Prince dozed, Astrid made a tiny hole in the cup.

'This time, I want to spill some magic,' she said. 'It's the only way to wake him. Long Nose is so greedy, I'll give her the golden spinning wheel for one last visit.'

Long Nose agreed at once.

'What do I care?' she said. 'Tomorrow the Prince and I will be married.'

At bedtime, Long Nose didn't spot the tiny hole as she filled the silver cup. Nor did she spot the magic drink leaking out.

Later, after Long Nose had gone, it was easy for Astrid to wake the Prince.

'Astrid!' the Prince exclaimed. 'Have you come to save me?'

'If I can,' Astrid said. 'But how do we get rid of Long Nose?'

'With a test of true love,' said the Prince. 'The winner will be the one who can clean the magic wax from my shirt. That's the person I'll marry!'

At first, Long Nose was very cross. But she was far too proud to say no to the test.

'Anybody can wash a shirt!' she sneered. 'Bring me a tub, some soap, and a scrubbing brush.'

Long Nose had spoken much too soon. The harder she scrubbed, the blacker the shirt became. In the end she screeched, 'Help me, trolls!'

Every troll in the castle came running. But the shirt got blacker and blacker.

'Stop scrubbing!'
Long Nose yelled.
'Let Astrid try. How
can a girl like her
beat trolls like us?'

With true love, that's how.

Astrid dipped the Prince's shirt in some cool, clear water. Instantly, it was as white as snow again.

Long Nose and her team of trolls were beaten. They were never seen again, not even east of the sun and west of the moon. Everybody else was invited to the royal wedding; family, friends, the three hags, and the four winds as well.

Afterwards, the gold and silver castle appeared again and Astrid and her Prince went back to their home. There they lived happily ever after.

What can be more magical than that?

The sea is beautiful, powerful, and unpredictable, full of mystery and danger—and this makes it a perfect setting for exciting stories. This Scottish myth of the Selkie has been told for centuries by people who lived their lives by the sea, looking out at the waves as seals played in the water—so it's easy to see where the idea of the Selkie came from.

The
Selkie

Retold by Malachy Doyle

Illustrated by Victoria Assanelli

Every evening William took a walk down to the beach. He lived on an island, far out in the northern sea, and all sorts of treasures washed up on its shores.

But one night he saw an amazing sight. By the light of the midsummer moon, a group of sea-people were dancing on the sand!

When they spotted him, they ran for their seal-
skins, pulled them on, and plunged into the water.
But one wasn't quick enough. William grabbed
the seal-skin before she could reach it.

'No!' cried the sea-maiden. 'Oh please!' she said, begging him to give it back.

But she was far more beautiful than anyone William had ever seen. And, although he knew it was unkind to keep her seal-skin, he couldn't bear to let the sea-maiden go.

'Come with me,' he said, wrapping his coat around her.

When they arrived at his cottage,
William sat the girl by the fire and
brought her food and drink. Then,
while she was eating, he slipped out to
hide her seal-skin.

The selkie, for so she was, knew that she had to stay. For without her salty seal-skin, she could never return to the ocean.

She never gave up hope, though, that one day William would give it back to her. Then she could go home, to the welcoming sea.

In time, she and William were married, and in time they had three sons. They were just like any other boys, apart from the fact that each had a flap of skin, like a web, between their fingers. And another between their toes.

Every evening the sea-maiden went down to the shore. As she sang to the seals, they came in close to listen.

But she never set foot in the sea, for without her salty seal-skin she knew she couldn't last long in the frozen waters.

One morning, while William was out fishing, the sea-maiden decided to mend some broken nets.

She went to the boathouse and pulled a dusty net down from a high shelf.

But as it tumbled into her hands, she saw . . .

Her seal–skin!

With a cry of joy, she held it to her face and breathed in the salt-smell of the ocean.

Then she ran home and hid it under the bed.

That evening, having fed them an excellent meal, she kissed her husband and her three fine sons.

'I'm going down to the shore,' she said.

But she didn't tell them what she was wearing under her clothes.

For she'd found her salty seal-skin,
and the ocean . . . the ocean was calling.

'At last!' she cried, tearing her clothes off and plunging
into the ice-cold water. 'I'm coming home!'

And every seal, from miles around,
came to join her.

Glancing back to shore, one final time, the sea-maiden saw her husband and sons, rushing down to the beach.

'Don't go, my bonny lass!' cried William. 'Please don't leave us!'

But, though the sea-maiden loved them one and all, she had no choice.

'I have given you the best years of my life, dear
husband,' she called out, over the waves. 'But I am a
selkie, a creature of the sea—and now that the salt is back
in my blood, I shall never go back to land!'

And with that, she dived beneath the
waves and was gone.

In this eerie German legend, the town of Hamelin is completely overrun by rats. A mysterious stranger offers to help for a fee, but when the work is done, the town refuses to pay him what he's owed. The pied piper decides to punish the town for its dishonesty, but is he right to do so?

This story, like *The Frog Prince*, teaches us about the importance of keeping a promise, and sticking to an agreement. As you read through the other stories in this collection, see if you can spot other times where promises are made or broken.

The Pied Piper

Retold by Adèle Geras

Illustrated by Ian Beck

Nobody knew where they'd come from, but one day the rats were there. Some people said they lived in the mud along the banks of the river Weser, which ran through the town of Hamelin. Others thought they had come from the forests which grew on the hills nearby.

The rats were everywhere. They ran down alleyways and up drainpipes. They scampered over floors, tap-tapping on the wood with their black claws.

They trailed their pink, rubbery tails through the food in every larder. They gathered under beds and went to sleep between the sheets in the chests of drawers. They climbed into cots where babies lay dreaming. By candlelight, their eyes were like red points of fire in the darkness.

The people of Hamelin were happy and busy before the rats came to the town. The baker baked bread and cakes. The butcher's meat pies were famous for their flavour.

The grocer made the tastiest pickles for miles
around. Everyone was polite and smiling and
said 'Good morning' to their neighbours as
they passed them in the street.

But now, the people of Hamelin were
in despair.

'It's a disaster!' they cried. 'Those rats
are bigger than cats. Someone should
do something.'

The mayor called a meeting. 'These rats,' he said, 'are a plague on our town. Can no one trap them or poison them?'

'We've tried,' said one man, 'but there are always more rats.'

'Fatter rats,' said a woman.

'Rats with sharper teeth,' added an old man.

Then a voice spoke from the back of the room. 'I will do it.'

Everyone turned to see who had spoken.

A man stood just inside the door. In one hand he held a silver flute and his clothes were half red and half yellow.

He spoke again. 'I can rid Hamelin

of its rats, but my price is a thousand gold coins.'

'Thank you, kind sir,' said the mayor, and everyone
clapped.
'A thousand gold coins will be yours, if you really can
do what you've promised.'

The man nodded and left the room. Everyone
followed him out to the main street and watched to see
what would happen next.

The man put the flute to his lips and began to play
as he walked away down the street. Then, from every
house the rats came running. A river of rats raced to
follow the Pied Piper's silvery tune.

They filled the road from pavement to pavement in a moving carpet of black and brown and pale grey fur. And when the piper reached the Weser, the rats plunged down the bank and into the river. The icy water closed over their furry heads. Every one of them was drowned.

When the townspeople looked for the Pied Piper, they couldn't find him.

As the days went by, they wondered what had become of him. After a few weeks, everyone had forgotten all about the rats.

Then one day, the Pied Piper returned to Hamelin. He walked into a meeting at the Town Hall. The mayor said, 'Greetings, friend. We wondered where you were.'

'I have come to collect the thousand gold coins you promised me.'

The mayor laughed. 'A thousand coins? My dear fellow! A hundred, surely? It's ridiculous to expect a thousand gold coins for one piece of work.'

'The rats are dead, sir. They have left your town. That was my work. Without me, Hamelin would still be overrun with the filthy creatures.'

'Take a hundred coins or take nothing,' said the mayor.

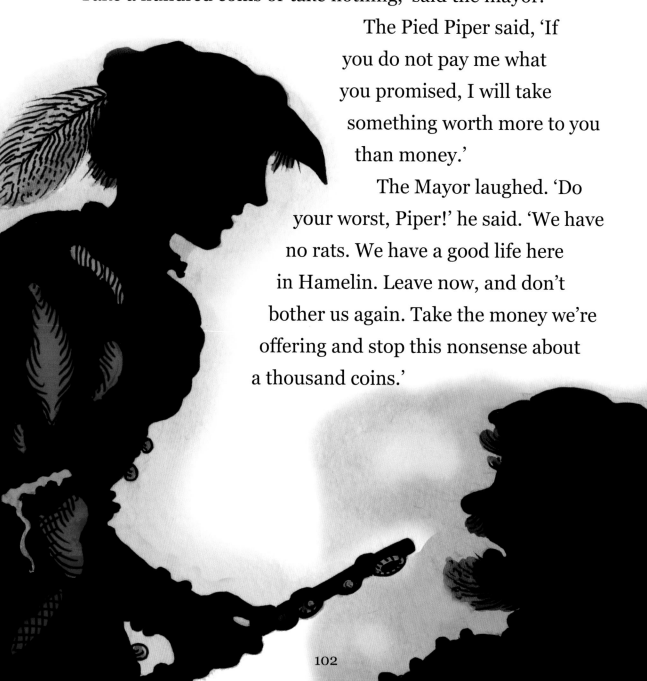

The Pied Piper said, 'If you do not pay me what you promised, I will take something worth more to you than money.'

The Mayor laughed. 'Do your worst, Piper!' he said. 'We have no rats. We have a good life here in Hamelin. Leave now, and don't bother us again. Take the money we're offering and stop this nonsense about a thousand coins.'

The Pied Piper left the room. The mayor felt pleased with himself. He had saved the town a great deal of money.

For a few days, life in Hamelin continued pleasantly enough. The men and women of the town went about their business. The mayor strutted around the main square, smiling and bowing when people thanked him for ridding the town of rats.

Summer had come to the world and the river glittered in the sunlight. The children of Hamelin were happy in the open air, playing games: running, skipping, kicking a ball across the grass, and making dens along the riverbank. Everyone had forgotten about the Pied Piper.

Then one day, the Pied Piper appeared in the town again. On market day, he was sitting on the edge of the fountain in the main square. The mayor was taking his morning walk, and saw him.

'You again!' the mayor said, marching up to the young man in the strange clothes. 'I thought we'd seen the last of you.'

The Pied Piper stood up, took off his red and yellow hat, and bowed to the mayor. 'I am waiting for my thousand gold coins,' he said.

'Wait as long as you like,' said the mayor. 'You won't be getting any more gold coins from this town, I promise you.'

The Pied Piper put his hat on again.

'As you wish,' he said. He turned his back on the mayor and began to walk across the square, making his way out of the town.

The Pied Piper turned into a dark alley, and
then he took out his flute and began to play.

The tune was a simple melody, as sweet and golden
as melted sugar. It twisted into the air and spread
out into every corner of the town.

Every man and woman in Hamelin stood quite still, as though they'd been bewitched. But the children . . . oh! The children were pulled towards it as if by a magnet. They had to follow, had to leave everything they had ever known, and follow the Pied Piper on and on.

The Pied Piper led the children through the streets of Hamelin, and out past the last house, and over the furthest field, and through the wood at the edge of the town.

All the children of Hamelin followed the Pied Piper through the wood to the foot of a dark mountain.

They forgot everything: their parents and
teachers, their homes and their beds,
their toys and games, and everyone and
everything they loved.

But one child could not go with them. John, on his crutches, was too slow to keep up with his friends. When the townspeople came looking for their children, John was there at the side of the road, crying.

'Where are the children?' the mayor cried. A crowd
of parents was there too, weeping for their sons and
daughters. 'What has become of them?'

'The Pied Piper has taken them into the mountain,' said John. 'I tried to follow, but before I got there, they had gone.'

'How can that be?' said one woman. 'They must be on the mountain.'

'No,' said John. 'A hole opened up like a huge door in the side of the mountain and they all went in, following the Pied Piper.'

'And then? What happened then?'

Everyone stood in silence as John started to cry.

'The gap in the side of the mountain closed up. They
are there now, inside the mountain. Locked there
forever,' said John. He burst into tears and everyone
wept with him.

The Pied Piper was never seen in Hamelin ever again.

Cinderella is one of the oldest and best-known fairy tales in the world, and no magical story collection would be complete without it. It's a rags-to-riches story, so at the beginning Cinderella has nothing, but with the help of a little magic her fortunes change completely. Can you think of other stories you've read in this collection that are similar?

Cinderella

Retold by Julia Jarman

Illustrated by Galia Bernstein

Once upon a time, there was a girl called Cinderella. She had a loving father, but he was often away. Her stepmother didn't like her, nor did her bad-tempered stepsisters.

118

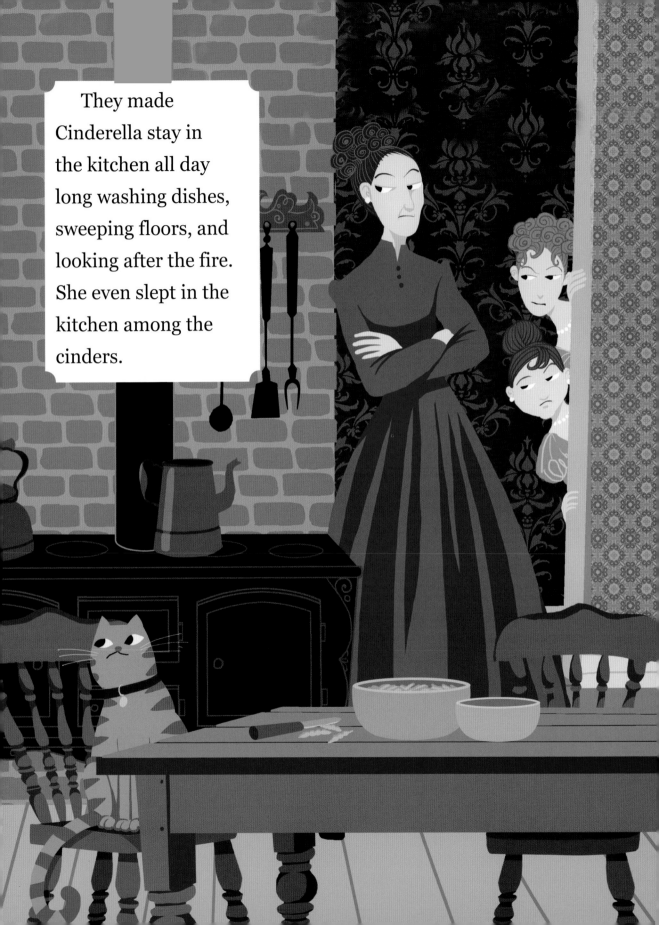

They made Cinderella stay in the kitchen all day long washing dishes, sweeping floors, and looking after the fire. She even slept in the kitchen among the cinders.

One day, they came running into the kitchen.

'Look, Cinderella, an invitation from the King!' cried the sulky one.

'We're going to a ball!' cried the stroppy one.

'At the palace!'

'Us, not you,' they added, smirking.

They began to argue about shoes and dresses. They were still arguing on the night of the ball when poor Cinderella had to help them get dressed.

When they had gone, she couldn't help feeling sad.

'I wish I could go to the ball,' she sighed. Suddenly the gloomy kitchen lit up . . .

FLASH!

'You can, my dear!'
Looking up, Cinderella saw a kind old lady.
'W-what? Who are you?'

'I'm your fairy godmother,' said the old lady, 'and I say you can go to the ball.'

'But how?' cried Cinderella.
'In a coach of course!' the fairy godmother laughed.

She sent Cinderella into the garden to get a pumpkin.
Then she waved her magic wand. **FLASH!**

The pumpkin turned into a golden coach!

'Now we need horses,' said the fairy godmother.
'Let these mice out of the cage, please.'

Cinderella did as she was told. The fairy godmother
waved her wand and . . .

Four white horses stood before the golden coach!

'Now,' said the fairy godmother, pointing her wand at the cat. 'All you need is a jolly coachman!'

FLASH!

'Now you can go to the ball!' she cried.

'But ...' Cinderella looked down at her old clothes. 'What about my dress?'

'Oh!' laughed the fairy godmother. 'I nearly forgot!'

She waved her wand again and . . .

FLASH!

Looking down, Cinderella saw the most beautiful dress she had ever seen.

'Put these on too,' said the fairy godmother, giving her a pair of slippers.

Made of glass, they fitted perfectly.

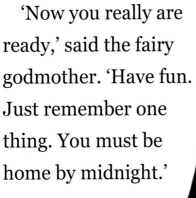

'Now you really are ready,' said the fairy godmother. 'Have fun. Just remember one thing. You must be home by midnight.'

'When the clock strikes twelve all my magic will end. Your coach will turn back into a pumpkin and your beautiful clothes will once again be rags.'

'I will remember!' cried Cinderella, as she climbed eagerly into the coach. 'Thank you very much!'

Then the coachman flicked
his whip and the horses
galloped into the starry night.

Meanwhile, on the steps of the palace, the Prince was bored.
So many coaches. So many princesses. So many people to greet.
Then another coach pulled up and . . .

. . . out stepped Cinderella.

'Who is she?' he asked, for he had never seen anyone so lovely.

But no one could tell him. No one knew who she was, not even her stepsisters.

133

The stepsisters did not recognize Cinderella, even when they got close, but they did feel jealous.

'Why does the Prince not look at us?' they cried.

For the Prince looked only at Cinderella.

'Why does he not dance with us?' they cried, when the Prince asked Cinderella to dance again and again for he had fallen in love with her.

As for Cinderella,
she could hardly believe
what was happening
. . . a handsome prince
was dancing with her!

She was so happy
that she forgot the
fairy godmother's
warning, even
when the clock
started to strike
midnight.

One! Two! Three!

She danced on ...

Four! Five! Six!

She danced on ...

Seven! Eight! Nine!

Suddenly she remembered and began to run towards the door.

'Come back! Come back!' called the Prince, but Cinderella kept on running.

Ten!

She reached the door and ran down the steps as fast as she could. One of her slippers fell off, but still she kept running.

Eleven!

'Come back! Come back!' She heard the Prince calling as she looked around wildly.

Twelve!

'Where are my coach and horses?' she cried.

Sadly she began to walk home, back to the kitchen.
'I'll never see the Prince again,' she sighed.

Meanwhile, the Prince was determined to find the beautiful princess with whom he had fallen in love.

'Tomorrow I will search every house in the land until I find the owner of this glass slipper,' he cried. 'Then I will marry her.'

Early next day, he
set off with his page
to begin the search.
It was evening when
they came to the house
where Cinderella lived.

The stepsisters were
waiting.
'Me first!' screamed one.
'No me!' cried the other.
First one, then the other,
tried to get her foot into the
slipper.

'Sorry,' said the page.
'Yours is too wide and yours is too
long. Does anyone else live here?'

'Me,' said Cinderella, who had come in quietly. 'Could I try?'

'YOU?' laughed the stepsisters. 'Get back to the kitchen!'
But they were too late.

The page put the slipper on Cinderella's foot and it was a perfect fit!

The Prince was gazing at her full of love.

'Will you marry me?' he said.

'Yes,' said Cinderella, who could see that he loved her even in rags.

The Prince was as kind as he was handsome. Cinderella was as happy as she ever thought she could be.

So they were married and lived together till the end
of their days in perfect harmony.

If you could wish for anything, what would it be? It's always tricky to word wishes, and in this old folktale, a couple make a wish to have a son, even if he's no bigger than a thumb. Well, that's exactly what they get, a thumb-sized-boy called Tom. But being tiny isn't a problem at all for Tom—in fact, it leads to all sorts of enormous adventures.

Tom Thumb

Retold by Jeanne Willis

Illustrated by Nicolás Aznárez

In the days of King
Arthur, there was
a magician called Merlin.
Once, he went
travelling dressed as a
beggar. Along the way, he
saw a farmer and begged
him for food.

The farmer and his wife gave Merlin milk and bread. They were good to him, but they looked unhappy.

'Why are you so sad?' asked Merlin.

'We have no children,' said the farmer.

'I would love a son, even if he was no bigger than my thumb,' said his wife.

Merlin granted her wish.

Soon after, the farmer's wife had a son. He was so tiny that they called him Tom Thumb.

Tom Thumb was little, but he got into big trouble. When the farmer's wife made a cake, he fell into the mixture.

She did not see him there, and almost cooked him!

One day, a raven flew off with Tom Thumb.

It dropped him in the sea and a big fish chased him.

Tom tried to swim away, but the fish swallowed him in one gulp!

'Hey ho, it's very dark in here,' said Tom. 'Never mind. I will have a nap.'

The fish was caught and taken to the castle. When the cook cut it open, out came Tom!

'Goodness! This boy is no bigger than my thumb!' said King Arthur.

He gave Tom his own little chair . . . his own little palace . . . and his own little coach pulled by six mice!

But the Queen was jealous of Tom Thumb. She was so mean, Tom hid from her in a snail shell.

Then a butterfly flew by. Tom Thumb jumped on its back.

The Queen's knights chased the butterfly.

At last, Tom fell off and they caught him.

'Cut off his head!' said the Queen.

'Not now, dear,' said King Arthur.

'Do it tomorrow then!' she said.

Poor Tom was put in a mousetrap.

In the night, a cat came. The cat thought Tom was a mouse and broke the trap.

Tom fed the cat the cheese from the trap and was free!

He did a dance of joy round the castle ballroom.

When the Queen saw him jigging about, she laughed out loud.

'Tom Thumb! However did you get free?' she said.

'I kept my head, Your Majesty!'
he said.

He was so funny and
brave and clever, the
Queen forgave him.

Tom Thumb lived in his little palace for the rest of his days.

Not many people could make the Queen laugh,
but he did. If the Queen was happy, King Arthur was happy.

Tom Thumb may have been little, but he had a great
big smile.

Which is why everyone in the kingdom loved him
enormously!

As we saw in the previous story, wishes are often at the heart of magical tales. In this Japanese story, Yoshi the stonecutter makes a lot of wishes, always wanting to be something else, something better, something more powerful. But along the way he learns that the only way he can really be happy is if he learns to value what he already has.

Yoshi the Stonecutter

Retold by Becca Heddle

Illustrated by Meg Hunt

Long ago in the mountains of Japan, there lived a stonecutter called Yoshi. He was a poor man with a bent back and hard hands from cutting stone.

People said a spirit lived in the
mountains where Yoshi worked.
They said it granted wishes.

But Yoshi had never seen the spirit.

One day, Yoshi took some stone to a rich man's house. Yoshi loved the rich man's beautiful home, his silk clothes, and his clean, soft hands.

'Oh, I wish I could be a rich man,' whispered Yoshi.
A cool wind blew and the mountain spirit appeared.
It whispered, 'Your wish is granted, Yoshi—a rich man
you now shall be.'

When Yoshi got home, his hut had become
a fine house.

Yoshi was rich. He put away his tools and rested,
looking out of the window.

The day grew hot. Yoshi saw a prince ride by.

Servants fanned the prince to cool him, and shaded
him with golden umbrellas.

'I wish I could be a prince,' said Yoshi.

The spirit said, 'Your wish is granted, Yoshi—a prince you now shall be.'

Now Yoshi was a prince, riding in a carriage with servants around him.

Prince Yoshi smiled as he sheltered from the sun
under golden umbrellas. His servant gave him water in
a jewelled cup and Yoshi happily sipped it.

Prince Yoshi soon felt very
hot—even the umbrellas didn't help.
When he splashed water on his skin,
the hot sun soon dried it up.

'The sun is more powerful than
me,' muttered Yoshi. 'I wish I could
be the sun.'
The spirit spoke again. 'Your wish
is granted, Yoshi—the sun you now
shall be.'

168

Yoshi felt himself rise into the sky and start to shine. He really was the sun! He sent his powerful rays down to Earth.

Yoshi shone harder. He made people sweat and burned their skin. He dried out the land and made the grass wither. Everything could feel his power.

171

One day, Yoshi the sun could not see the ground. A cloud was in his way. He shone with all his might, but the cloud would not go.

'Can a cloud blot out my power?' cried Yoshi.
'Then I wish I could be a cloud.'

'Your wish is granted, Yoshi—a cloud you
now shall be,' replied the spirit.

Yoshi became a big, thick
grey cloud. He shut out the
sun's heat and shaded the
people. He cooled the land,
and then he began to rain.

Yoshi's rain made streams
and rivers flow, and made
puddles on the ground. The
grass soon turned green again
and the crops began to grow.

Yoshi the cloud rained harder and harder. In the mountains, the little streams became great waterfalls. Rivers overflowed and drowned the crops.

The flood water came rushing down roads and poured into villages. Only the huge rocks on the mountains stood firm and would not move.

177

'Rocks are more powerful than clouds,' grumbled Yoshi. 'I wish I could be a rock.'

The spirit replied, 'Your wish is granted, Yoshi—a rock you now shall be.'

Now Yoshi was a rock—huge, hard,
and solid.
　He did not fear the sun or the rain.
'Nothing can be stronger
than me,' he boasted.

Then Yoshi the rock felt tools cutting into him.

'A stonecutter is stronger than me!' said Yoshi.

'I wish I could be a man again.'

The mountain spirit smiled. 'Your wish is granted,

Yoshi—a man you now shall be.'

Yoshi the stonecutter picked up his tools and started to work.
His back was bent and he was poor— but now he was happy.

This story features a strange little goblin with an extremely unusual name. His origins come from German folklore, where small creatures called 'Rumpelstilts' made noises by rattling sticks or posts. As annoying as noisy goblins are, they don't sound as wicked or meddling as the villain in this story, who strikes a bargain that he knows can't be kept.

Rumpelstiltskin

Retold by Joanna Nadin

Illustrated by Alejandro O'Keeffe

In the far off times, there lived a poor miller and his daughter, Lily. Lily was kind and clever and good, but the miller was a show-off, who liked to tell tall tales.

Lily was in love with a prince, but was too poor to be his wife.
So the miller went to the King and boasted about his daughter.
'She can spin straw into pure gold,' he said.

The King was delighted and summoned Lily to the
castle. There, he took her to a turret and showed her a
bale of straw.

'Spin it into gold by morning and you may marry my son,'
he said. Then he locked the door.

But, of course, Lily had no idea what to do, and stamped her foot crossly. At this sound, a goblin appeared.

'Give me your necklace and I will spin the straw into gold,' he said.

Lily's necklace had belonged to her mother, so she did
not want to give it away. Yet she did want to marry the
Prince, so she agreed. The goblin was as good as his word
and spun the straw into reels of gold.

The King was pleased, but he was also greedy. He took
Lily to another turret with two bales of straw.

'Spin it into gold by morning and you may marry my
son,' he said. Then he locked the door.

Again Lily stamped her foot, and again the goblin appeared.

'Give me your ring and I will spin the straw into gold for you,' he said.

Lily gave him the ring and the goblin spun the straw into reels of gold.

The King smiled when he saw the gold, but it made
him greedier still.

He took Lily to another turret with three bales of straw.
'Spin it into gold by morning and you may marry my
son,' he said. Then he locked the door.

Again Lily stamped her foot and again the goblin appeared.

'I have nothing left to give you,' she said.
'But I need your help.'

So the goblin thought, and replied, 'Give me your first child and I will spin the straw into gold.'

Lily, who did not much care for babies, agreed and the
goblin spun the straw into reels of gold. This time, the
King kept his word and Lily married the Prince.

The years passed, and in her happiness, Lily forgot that she did not much care for babies. She and the Prince had a little boy. They called him Tom.

Lily also forgot her promise to the goblin. But the goblin
did not forget. On Tom's first birthday, he came to the castle
and said, 'Give me your baby.'

Lily could not bear to be parted from Tom, and offered
the goblin gold instead. But the goblin said Tom was the
only treasure he wanted.

But, as I have told you, Lily was a clever girl.

'If I can guess your name, will you let me keep Tom?' she said.

'I will give you three days,' said the goblin. 'But you will not win. The child will be mine.'

Lily set to work. On the first day she wrote down all the boys' names she had heard of. When the goblin came that evening, she said, 'Is your name Adam?'

'No,' smiled the goblin. 'That is not my name.'

'Is it Ahmed?' asked Lily.

'No,' smiled the goblin.

'That is not my name.'

Lily tried Akeem and Anton and Hassan and Hans.
Each time the goblin said the same thing.
'No, that is not my name.'

On the second day Lily went to the castle library, and wrote down all the boys' names she hadn't heard of.

When the goblin came that evening, she said, 'Is your name Achilles?'

'No,' smiled the goblin. 'That is not my name.'

'Is it Axel?' asked Lily.

'No,' smiled the goblin. 'That is not my name.'

Lily tried Careem and Caspar, and Santos and Solomon.
Each time the goblin said the same thing.

'No, that is not my name.'

On the third day Lily had run out of ideas. So she went for a long walk into town.

She walked around the market, listening out for anyone with a different name.

The only names she found in the market were ones she had already tried, like James, Jack, and Jonas. Lily had almost given up hope when she saw a market stall selling reels of thread.

A little man was
singing to himself as he
stacked them in neat
piles.

He sang:

'My name's not John,
My name's not Jim,
My name is
Rumpelstiltskin.'

Lily smiled, because
she could see that the
little man was the very
same goblin who wanted
to take Tom away.

When the goblin came that evening, she pretended not to know.

'Is your name Gumboot?' she said.

'No,' smiled the goblin. 'That is not my name.'

'Is it Marmalade?' asked Lily.

'No,' smiled the goblin. 'That is not my name.'

Lily tried Slurp and Squelch, and Mutton and Tintin.

But each time the goblin said the same thing.

'No, that is not my name.'

Then Lily had one last guess.

'Is your name Rumpelstiltskin?' she asked.

The goblin stamped his foot so hard it went
through the floor. He pulled with all his might but he
was stuck fast.

Lily offered to help him, as long as he vanished forever.

The angry goblin disappeared.
Tom stayed in the castle with Lily and
the Prince, and for all I know,
they are living there still.

Magical stories sometimes take their characters into amazing worlds through doors, portals, or underwater. In this German folktale, twelve princesses travel to a secret world every night through a wardrobe! Have you ever wondered what doors to magical worlds might be hiding in your everyday world?

Twelve Dancing Princesses

Retold by Geraldine McCaughrean

Illustrated by Bee Willey

Tramper could feel the stony road through the holes in his boots. A newspaper blew by, Tramper picked it up and sat down to cover the holes in his boots with the paper.

A frail old lady glared and stared at him.

'You think you have shoe troubles!' she said. 'The King has twelve girls and all of them have holes in their slippers!'

The old lady's feet were bare, cut and purple with cold. Tramper felt sorry for her, so he gave her his shabby boots. To thank him, she gave Tramper her dirty cloak. As she clumped away down the road, she called:

'Stay awake.

Drink no drop.

Sip no sup.

Taste no cup.'

'An odd way to say goodbye,' thought Tramper.

Rain drizzled down. Tramper put on the cloak and tried to read what was left of the wet newspaper. As it fell apart in his hands he read:

PALACE NOTICE

WANTED:

Answer to the Mystery of the Worn Slippers.

REWARD:

Princess' hand in marriage.

SNAG:

All those who fail will be locked up.

'Why not?' thought
Tramper.
'I bet I could solve the
mystery. I've got nothing
to lose, I don't even have
any boots.' And, when he
looked down, his feet were
gone too. His feet, legs,
and body had gone. He
was invisible. 'The cloak is
magic!' he gasped.

The King's twelve daughters were a mystery. Each night they slipped off their silk slippers and went to bed. But each morning their silk slippers were full of holes, and the girls were worn out.

How could it happen? The girls' bedroom door was locked, so they could not get out.

How could it go on? The King was spending all his money on slippers!

221

Princes came from everywhere to solve the mystery. Each stood watching the princesses as they slept. Each tried to keep awake by choosing which one of the princesses he would marry. But the next morning he woke up on the couch, surrounded by sleeping princesses and twenty-four holey slippers. And after the third time, the royal guard threw him into prison.

Princes stopped coming and knights came instead, then squires. They were all determined to solve the mystery, but they all failed.

The King was furious. New slippers had to be bought every day. The prisons were full to bursting with princes, knights, and squires. But Tramper didn't know any of this.

Tramper went to the castle and stood before the King.

'You have no boots!' said the King in deep disgust.

'And you keep running out of slippers,' said Tramper.

The princesses were kind to Tramper. 'A brave man deserves a good supper,' they said, and brought him baked salmon and a glass of milk. He ate the salmon but remembering the advice of the old lady, he did not drink one drop of milk. Secretly, he let the cat drink the milk, until, with a miaow, it fell off the window sill, sound asleep.

'So that's the trick!' thought Tramper.

The princesses went to bed and Tramper
lay down on the couch. He snored loudly,
pretending to sleep.

Later that night . . . the distant sound of a
strange music began. The princesses jumped
out of bed and slipped their feet into their
brand new slippers. Then they all climbed
into the wardrobe!

The princesses pushed between the hanging clothes and ran down a passageway. Tramper followed them with the old lady's magic cloak over his head. The princesses ran across a garden of ruby roses, through an orchard of diamond fruit, and up some glass steps towards a magnificent castle. Tramper ran after them.

The princesses twirled into a great hall. There, waiting for
them were twelve shadowy shapes. Twelve elves. Tramper
watched as they danced. The elves' shoes were hard, but the
soles of the silken slippers were soon worn thin.

'So that's the trick!' said Tramper.

Before dawn, twelve very tired girls in worn-out slippers
went back to bed. Tramper hurried ahead of them and lay
down on the couch.

There the King found him, surrounded by tattered
slippers, snoring loudly. 'Well?'

You might think that Tramper told the King
about what he had seen, but no. He had
enjoyed the salmon so much that he was
hoping for a second supper.

'Two more tries,' said the King.
'That's all!'

The next night, the princesses brought Tramper turkey and a cup of tea for his supper. He gobbled down the turkey but *sipped no sup.* He gave the palace parrot his tea and it fell off its perch, sound asleep.

The princesses and Tramper fell asleep, too – or so it seemed. Later that night . . . the distant sound of silvery music began. The twelve princesses jumped out of bed, into the wardrobe, and ran across the garden of ruby roses, through the orchard of diamond fruit, and up the glass steps into the castle. Tramper followed them with the magic cloak over his head.

Again the elves were waiting. Again the princesses danced
and danced until their slippers were ragged.

Before dawn, the princesses made their weary way home.
Tramper hurried ahead of them and lay down on the couch.

There the King found him, surrounded by tattered slippers,
snoring loudly. 'Well?'

You might think that Tramper told the King about what he
had seen, but no. He had enjoyed the turkey so much that he
was hoping for a third supper.

'One more night,' said the King, '. . . and what's wrong with
the parrot?'

The next night, the princesses brought him chicken pie and a glass of water. He swallowed down the pie but he did not drink or sip or even taste the water.

He poured the water into a vase and the roses drooped their sleepy heads.

'Your time is up,' said the King the next morning, when he found Tramper asleep on the couch. Two dozen slippers lay, worn out, around him.

Do you think Tramper put on his magic cloak and ran? No. Do you think he told the unbelievable truth? He did.

'I followed your daughters through their wardrobe, into a garden of ruby roses and an orchard of diamond fruit, to a castle of magical elves where they danced and danced until the soles of their slippers wore thin.'

'Liar!' said the princesses.

'Rubbish!' said the King.

'I can prove it,' said Tramper and put his hand into his pocket and pulled out one ruby rose and one diamond pear. 'Shall I nail the wardrobe shut, Your Majesty, before your daughters are danced away?'

'Clever man!' roared the King. 'Marry my oldest daughter! Then one day you will be king!'

But Tramper chose the youngest, because she was the best dancer.

There was lots of dancing at the wedding, all of it barefoot. Then everyone put on their silken shoes and went home, as happy as can be.

Like many of the stories in this collection, the English folktale of Jack and the Beanstalk existed long before it was first written down; it would have been passed on from one storyteller to the next for hundreds, maybe even thousands, of years. That's why sometimes there can be many different versions of the same fairy tale. In some versions of this story, Jack is a cunning trickster; in others a heroic daredevil; and in some a foolish boy. Maybe in this story he's a mix of all three. What do you think?

Back hundreds of years ago, some people would have believed in the magic of folktales like this, fearing witches and ogres, and putting faith into wishes and charms. Few people believe in magic today, but as Jack proves, if you're willing to chance on the impossible, the tiniest of opportunities, something truly magical can grow out of it.

Jack and the Beanstalk

Retold by Michael Morpurgo

Illustrated by Joanna Carey

My name is Jack Spriggins and this is my story.

When I was little everyone in the village called me Poor Boy Jack. And we were poor too, my Ma and I. Ma was never well. She ached in her bones and never had enough breath to breathe, but she always did her best to look after me. We lived in a little cottage, where the rain came in through the roof and the windows. We gathered what we could from the country round about, berries, nuts, mushrooms, herbs, grew a few potatoes and leeks in the garden, kept a speckledy hen for our eggs. It was never enough. In winter months we always went hungry. Without the milk and cheese from Milky-white, our lovely cow, we would have starved.

One night in a storm, the wind blew our chimney off, and half the roof as well. 'There's nothing else for it,' said Ma, 'we need to find the money to repair the roof before the winter comes, or we shall freeze to death. We shall have to sell Milky-white.' I begged her not to, but she would not listen. I loved that old cow. She didn't just give us her milk, she was like a friend to me. 'Off you go to the market tomorrow, Jack,' she told me. 'And mind you get the very best price you can for her.'

So the next morning, I went off down the lane with Milky-white. I didn't need a halter to lead her. I just had to talk to her, and she followed me wherever I went. I told her why we had to sell her, that we had no choice. 'I shan't sell you to some horrible farmer who won't look after you. I'll find someone kindly, I promise.'

After a while we came to the bridge by the wispy willow tree and I stopped to rest, and to let Milky-white drink in the stream. I was sitting there in the shade, when I saw an old man come hobbling down the lane, leaning heavily on his stick, and singing a happy tune.

'Morning, son,' he said with a cheery smile. 'Nice cow you got there. Gives you lots of nice creamy milk, does she?'

'Lots,' I replied. Then, and I don't know why, I told him the whole story, all about Milky-white and how she was the best cow in the world, and how the roof had been blown off in the storm and how Ma was poorly, and how I was off to market to sell Milky-white, and how sad I was to have to do it.

The old man listened to me intently. Then, after a moment's thought, he said: 'I have an idea. I like your cow, and I like you. So I will make you an offer.' He reached into the pocket of his raggedy coat, and produced three large beans. 'Now these are no ordinary beans, son. These are magic beans, enchanted beans, beans that will change your life for ever. All you've got to do is plant them. The rest is up to you. But be brave, Jack Spriggins, be brave, that is all I will say. Here's the deal then, your Milky-white for these enchanted beans, and for a faithful promise that I will look after your lovely cow for ever like a best friend. What do you say, son?'

Well, we all believe what we want to believe, don't we? My feet ached with walking, and there was still a long way to go to market. He looked like a kindly man, and if he was telling the truth about the enchanted beans, then all our problems could be solved, and how sweet life would be. It was too tempting. I said tearful goodbyes to Milky-white and walked back home, the beans in my hand, hoping all the way I had done the right thing. I was still wondering how this stranger had known my name when I arrived back home.

When I told Ma, and showed her the enchanted beans, she clearly did not think I had done the right thing at all. She went completely loopy. 'You sold our cow for a measly handful of beans!' she cried. 'How could you, Jack? That cow was all we had in this world.' In floods of tears, she snatched the beans off me, and hurled them out of the kitchen window. Then she sent me to my room in disgrace. She was crying downstairs and I was crying upstairs. How could I have been so stupid! Enchanted beans indeed! Idiot! Idiot!

We were so busy being upset, that we did not see the fox coming that evening and stealing away our only hen. All I found when I went to shut her up were the feathers. The cow was gone, the hen was gone, and Ma wasn't speaking to me. And as usual I was hungry when I went to bed that night. If I ever saw that old man again, I would give him a piece of my mind, that was for sure!

I woke up and it seemed the sun had not come up. I could hear birds singing, I knew it must be dawn but there was no sign of the rising sun. I soon saw why. Huge leaves were blocking out all the light at the window. I opened the window and looked out. Right in front of me was growing up out of the vegetable garden what looked at first like a towering tree, where there had been no tree. Then I saw that it was in fact not a tree at all, but a beanstalk, a gigantic beanstalk, with huge green leaves and a green trunk the breadth of an ancient oak tree. I looked up to see how high this tree went. I couldn't even see the top of it, it was hidden somewhere way up in the clouds.

I looked down, and then I remembered. Ma had
thrown the beans out of the kitchen window. This tree
was growing right outside the kitchen window. Those
beans were enchanted, so this gigantic beanstalk must be
enchanted too. How high did it go? Where would it lead?
Only one way to find out. But did I dare climb it? What
had the old man told me down by the stream?

'Be brave, Jack Spriggins, be brave.'

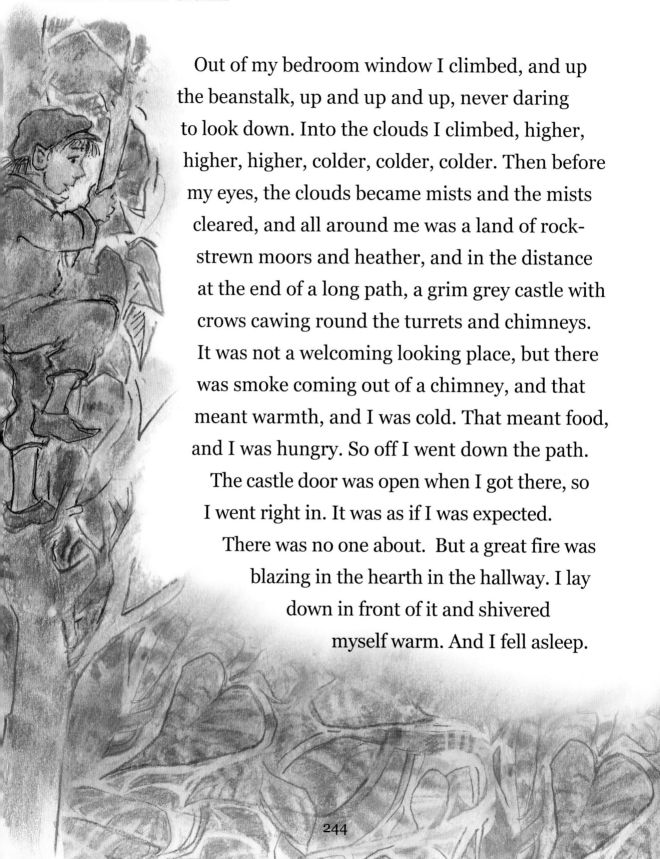

Out of my bedroom window I climbed, and up
the beanstalk, up and up and up, never daring
to look down. Into the clouds I climbed, higher,
higher, higher, colder, colder, colder. Then before
my eyes, the clouds became mists and the mists
cleared, and all around me was a land of rock-
strewn moors and heather, and in the distance
at the end of a long path, a grim grey castle with
crows cawing round the turrets and chimneys.
It was not a welcoming looking place, but there
was smoke coming out of a chimney, and that
meant warmth, and I was cold. That meant food,
and I was hungry. So off I went down the path.
The castle door was open when I got there, so
I went right in. It was as if I was expected.
There was no one about. But a great fire was
blazing in the hearth in the hallway. I lay
down in front of it and shivered
myself warm. And I fell asleep.

When I woke I found a lady kneeling over me,
shaking me awake. She had a sweet face, but
she was frightened of something, I could
see that at once. She kept looking over her
shoulder. 'You cannot stay here,' she
said. 'He may come back and find you.
Come away into the kitchen. Are you
hungry? Quickly, he may come home
any time.'

She led me down long dark
corridors and into the kitchen,
where she sat me down and fed
me as I had never been fed
before. A hot soup, a meat pie,
creamy chocolate cakes,
and to drink goblets of
apple juice. I thought
I had died and
gone to heaven.

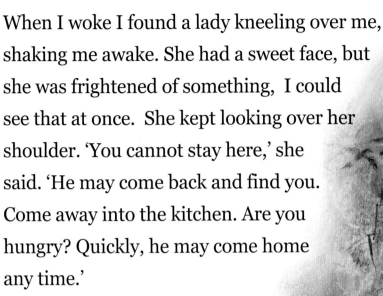

And all the time as I ate I told her who I was, told my story, and then she told me all about herself. She was called Glad. She had been carried away as a little girl years before, by a hideous monstrous ogre, called Gogmagog, who loved to eat children. But she had been too scrawny and thin to eat—he preferred eating boys, she said—so he had fed her up, and then had decided to keep her to look after him, to cook for him, clean for him, play the harp for him.

All he cared about besides eating children was gold. He loved gold. 'Look around you,' she said to me. And it was true, there was gold everywhere. Gold knives and forks and plates, a gold harp, and a chest in the corner full of gold coins. The place glittered with gold. 'And do you know how he gets all his gold? Over there in the cage. Do you see that golden hen? She lays him one golden egg every day.

He melts them down in the cellar and makes whatever he likes. Coins mostly. Every evening he sits there in that chair by the fire, and counts those coins.' Glad was wiping tears from her cheeks, 'and I have to play for him on the golden harp. How I hate him. How I long to run away. But there is no escape from this place. I have talked too much. If he finds you here, he will eat you for sure, and grind down your bones for bread. You must go, and go now.'

Just then I heard a great door slam and heavy footfalls coming along the corridor. 'Gogmagog!' she whispered. And then I heard a song, a terrible dreadful song, that sent shivers up my spine.

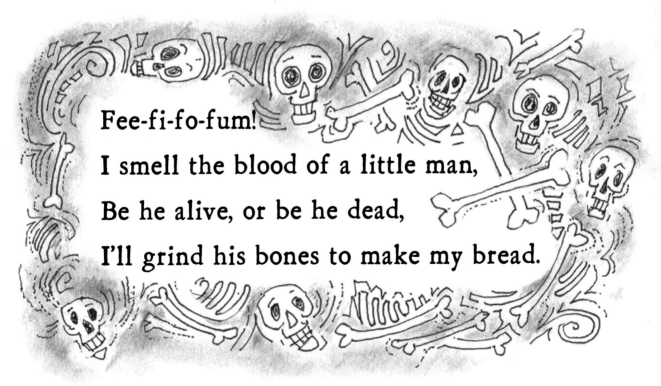

Fee-fi-fo-fum!
I smell the blood of a little man,
Be he alive, or be he dead,
I'll grind his bones to make my bread.

247

'Quick!' said Glad. 'Into the cupboard, and don't move, don't even breathe.' And with that she pushed me into the kitchen cupboard in amongst all the pots and pans. There I stayed for hours on end, listening to him eating and drinking, ordering her about, shouting at her, to do this, more meat, more wine; hurry, wench; more logs on the fire. Now play the harp, you wretched girl. Oh she played that harp so sweetly that it nearly lulled me to sleep in my cupboard. I only had to nudge one of those pots and pans, and I would be Gogmagog's next meal. How I struggled to stay awake.

Then, joy of joy, I heard through the gentle music of the harp, the sound of deep sonorous snoring. He was asleep, fast asleep. I kept quite still, until the cupboard door opened, and Glad helped me out, finger to her lips. We crept past the snoring Gogmagog, and he was as monstrous and hideous as I had imagined.

She led me by the hand to the kitchen door, opened it, kissed me tenderly on my forehead, and told me to go.

But I could not leave her there. One good turn deserves another I thought. And I had other ideas too. On tiptoe I went across the room, reached inside the cage, picked up the golden hen, and gave it to her. She held her, stroking her feathers, while I stuffed my pockets full of golden coins. Then with the golden harp under my arm we stole out of the castle kitchen together, leaving Gogmagog still snoring away by the fire.

Down the long corridor we ran, out of the great door of the castle, across the courtyard, and we were away. We both knew we were running for our lives. Never had I run so fast, and all the time the harp was heavier under my arm, and I could hear some of the coins falling out of my pockets. I did not stop to pick them up. And just as well I didn't, too. For we heard behind us the sound of Gogmagog coming after us, the earth shaking with his footfall, his roaring and raging echoing in our ears. He was coming closer and closer with every step. And like a war cry came his dreadful song:

Fee-fi-fo-fum! I smell the blood of a little man . . .

I tried not to listen, tried only to make my legs go faster. Ahead of us through the mist we saw at last the giant beanstalk, and down we climbed, me clinging to the golden harp, her with the golden hen clucking under her arm. We felt the

moment when Gogmagog
had reached the giant
beanstalk and was
climbing down above
us through the clouds.
The beanstalk shook as if
a hurricane was blowing,
shook us and shook us,
but we clung on and we
kept going down.

Then below I saw the
roof of our little cottage,
and Ma in the vegetable
garden looking up at us. I
called out to her, 'The axe, Ma.
Fetch the axe, quick, quick!' Above
us Gogmagog was still roaring in
his fury, and so close now I could
see the nails in his great boots. Then
we were down on the ground and Ma was
swinging the axe as hard as she could, but
she hadn't got the strength, I could see that. I
was too tired even to pick up the axe let alone

251

swing it. That was when Glad took the axe from Ma, handed her the hen, and set to work with the axe, swinging and chopping, and with every chop, she cried out another name, 'That's for Harry, that's for Moll, that's for Ben, that's for Billy, that's for Sam, that's for Shona . . .' And with every name the giant beanstalk shuddered, and began to topple. 'And that's for me!' Down came the beanstalk, Gogmagog with it, with a resounding crash. The ogre lay dead in the vegetable patch.

'That's ruined my leeks!' said Ma, laughing and crying at the same time, and hugging me to her. Then looking at Glad, she said, 'Welcome to our home. You saved my boy's life, so our home is your home for as long as you like.'

So that's my story. The three of us lived together, in a cottage with a new chimney and a new thatched roof, the golden hen laid her golden eggs every day, Glad played her harp, and she and Ma lived together like loving sisters, best of friends, as I grew up. Ma's aches and pains went right away. It was a glad day for us when Glad came to stay! As for me, I bought some fields and farmed the land, and all was well. I never saw again that old man who I met down by the stream that day. I wish I could, because I have a lot to thank him for. Whenever I cross the bridge on my way to market, I still thank him aloud. And I miss Milky-white to this day.

Ma and Glad and me, we still grow our potatoes and leeks in the vegetable garden, but never beans, never ever beans. One adventure like that in a lifetime is quite enough!

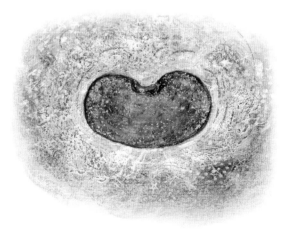

Acknowledgements

The following stories were commissioned for *TreeTops Greatest Stories*, *Myths and Legends,* and *Oxford Reading Tree Traditional Tales* collections and are reprinted by permission of the Author unless otherwise stated:

Authors

The Merman and The Selkie © Malachy Doyle 2016

The Pied Piper © Adèle Geras 2016

Sleeping Beauty © Pippa Goodhart 2016

The Frog Prince © Pippa Goodhart 2011

Yoshi the Stonecutter © Becca Heddle 2016

Cinderella © Julia Jarman 2011

Twelve Dancing Princesses © Geraldine McCaughrean 2011

Jack and the Beanstalk © Michael Morpurgo 2017

Rumpelstiltskin © Joanna Nadin 2011

East of the Sun, West of the Moon © Chris Powling 2011

Tom Thumb © Jeanne Willis 2016

Illustrators

The Merman and The Selkie © Victoria Assanelli 2016

Tom Thumb © Nicolás Aznárez 2016

The Pied Piper © Ian Beck 2016

Cinderella © Galia Bernstein 2011

Jack and the Beanstalk © Joanna Carey 2017

East of the Sun, West of the Moon © Violeta Dabija 2011

Yoshi the Stonecutter © Meg Hunt 2016

Rumpelstiltskin © Alejandro O'Keeffe 2011

The Frog Prince © Yannick Robert 2011

Sleeping Beauty © Bee Willey 2016

Twelve Dancing Princesses © Bee Willey 2011

Additional artwork and title typography © Nathan Collins